PRAISE FOR

TYLER & HIS SOLVE-A-MATIC MACHINE

"A heartwarming story of an orphan who goes through hardwork and determination to become an entrepreneur. "

-Jared, *age 11*

"My son ate this book up! What a terrific way to teach our children about free enterprise and stimulate their creativity."

–**Christine**, *mother of an 11-year old boy*

"I thought this book was a fun fantasy."

–Joseph, *age 12*

"I really like this book (sic) it was very exciting."

–Jennifer, *age 10*

"Judging from my daughter's reaction, you've got a winner here!...There are so many children's books on topics like 'How to handle anger' – most focus on feelings. Not many out there that touch on practical applications: things they can use day to day."

–**Terri**, *mother of a 10-year old girl*

"I would reccomend (sic) it to my friends who want to start a buisness (sic). "

–Alex, *age 9*

"If you like books read this one."

–Jake, *age 10*

Future Business Leaders' Series:

Tyler and His Solve-a-matic Machine

Jennifer Bouani

BOUJE
PUBLISHING

Atlanta

Published by
Bouje Publishing, LLC
1101 Juniper St., Suite 602, Atlanta, GA 30309
E-mail: jbouani@boujepublishing.com
To order: www.boujepublishing.com

Illustrated by
Guy Smalley, www.guysmalley.com

Edited by
Jennifer Shelley, Washington D.C.

ISBN: 0-9779265-0-8 (paperback)

Printed in the United States of America

Dedicated to the memory
of my father David Reaves
(1948-2002) and to my
daughter Avia Bouani.

May the
spirit of the entrepreneurs
pass through us
and
on to those
we leave behind.

ACKNOWLEDGEMENTS

I would like to thank...

My daughter Avia whose bright eyes and sweet smile give me a reason everyday to keep typing the lessons I learn.

The focus group kids & parents for your invaluable feedback: The Churches, The Capizzis, The McCanns, The Allisons, The Eidsons, and The Monsalves.

My editor, Jennifer Shelley, for not being shy about marking up the manuscript. Your objectivity really put the polish on it.

The La Lit book club members Rebecca Boyer and Aveline Hayes for not laughing at the first (and very laughable) draft and for providing great input.

George Largay, my mentor, for his wisdom on business, career, and networking.

My friends, family, and colleagues who contributed in their own ways: Jane Reaves, Stacey Cohen, Scott Drake, Lynn Morgan, Kara Yates, & Shawn Littlejohn.

My husband Hicham. You were the first to believe in this book. Without your expertise, hard work, and most of all, your passion, this book would not exist. "You Raise Me Up..."

"Go confidently in the direction of your dreams. Live the life you have imagined."

—Henry David Thoreau

TABLE OF CONTENTS

CHAPTER 1:
THE WISHBONE

Tyler Sogno tightly held his end of the wishbone. His buddy Jake held the other end. Jake closed his eyes to make his wish, but Tyler's eyes were wide open looking at a photo on his nightstand by his metal twin bed. Then Tyler looked to the wall above the photo. On it, he had proudly displayed his model sailboats. Just two days earlier, he had finished building one. It took months! Then he closed his eyes and concentrated on his memory of the photo. *I wish to be a sea captain one day, to sail around the world seeing all the countries, and to experience different cultures.*

Tyler opened his eyes, "Have you made your wish yet?"

Jake opened one eye, "No, one more minute."

Tyler whistled. Jake opened both eyes. "Do you mind? I'm trying to concentrate."

"I have to whistle. The story goes that sailors whistled in the dark to bring themselves good luck."

"But you're not a sailor."

"I will be," Tyler smiled, "—one day."

"And it's not dark."

"The sun is setting. It's close enough."

Jake closed his eyes again. Finally, twenty seconds later, he said, "OK, I'm ready."

As Tyler held his end of the wishbone, he was wishing for his dream to just happen—as most kids do when they make a wish over birthday candles; but when the bone snapped, a course was set in motion that would require much more of Tyler than he could ever have imagined.

"Tyler, I don't see your homework. Did you turn it in?"

Tyler stared back at his teacher Mother Marie. He did not remember any homework assignment due today. He frantically shuffled through his backpack.

"Tyler, did you hear me? Where is your report? It's not in this stack. Come here." Mother Marie thumbed through the papers on her desk.

Tyler slowly worked his way from his desk in the back of the classroom to his teacher's desk in the front, "Uh, I forgot about it, Mother Marie." Tyler bowed his head and looked down at his feet. *How could he be so stupid*, he thought.

He could hear Jake and his other friends outside laughing and playing. It was almost summer. Tyler loved summer in the city of Nessibus, but most of all he loved taking trips to nearby Sunrise Beach with the other kids in his orphanage. There he would splash around in the ocean and think about his father, the sailor.

Tyler did not know much about his father. He had that one photo of him next to his bed. His father had been the sea captain of a big boat. People would charter the boat to fish, travel to other ports, or just relax at sea. His father died while repairing the boat in the shipyard. It fell off its support and crushed him when Tyler was just a baby. The only relic Tyler had left of his father was a photo of him standing at the bow of the boat. He stood confidently with his dark beard and bronze skin. Tyler thought he looked like the strongest man he had ever seen.

"Tyler, I'm talking to you. You have to stop daydreaming and start paying attention in class. Turn your report in tomorrow. I'll have to deduct fifteen points for it being late, but that's better than a zero, right?"

"Yes, Mother Marie. I'm sorry. I promise I'll bring it to you tomorrow."

After dinner, Tyler sat at the small desk by the window in the study room of the orphanage. He tried to work on his homework assignment, but he kept staring out at the city skyline, a cluster of dark rectangle buildings with windows twinkling like Christmas tree lights. The Bay of Nessibus, reflecting the moonlight in the lapping waves, peeked through small breaks in the skyline. He watched the flashing, red light of a signal atop a skyscraper in the distance. *What goes* on in all of those buildings? So many companies. So many jobs. A rat scurried across the street below his window eight stories down.

When Tyler walked to school, he had to pass several of those tall office buildings. Usually Jake was with him, but one day when Jake was home sick, Tyler stopped and played on the steps of one of those tall office buildings. He watched business men and women coming and going from the building lobby. They were dressed in suits and carried laptop bags over their shoulders. Many were talking on their cell phones, probably discussing important business. Some stopped off at the coffee shop to get a cup of coffee before reporting to work. Others checked their watches then picked up their pace as they realized they were late for an important meeting.

That night while the other kids were working on their homework or playing down in the rec room, Tyler worked on his homework assignment alone in his room. A dusty moth fluttered through the window, buzzed past Tyler's ear, and landed on his desk lamp. Like Mother Marie standing at the chalkboard pointing at a math problem with her pointer, the light of the desk lamp cast a spotlight on his dreadful homework assignment. The memory of Mother Marie's voice rang in his ears, "*Tyler, I'm talking to you. You have to stop daydreaming and start paying attention...*"

He drew a sailboat in water with the sun shining on the horizon. "If only I had something to help me do my homework faster... Maybe I can talk Jake into helping me." He thought about that some more and realized Jake would rather be playing soccer than doing homework. Then, he thought about saving a portion of his lunch money everyday, and in a few days, buying the homework from Gene, the smart kid in class; however, after he calculated it, he found it would take him at least a month to save enough for just one homework assignment. Just when he was about to give up, it came to him, "...a machine that would take assignments, ask me questions, and spit out the completed assignment. That would be great. I would call it Solve-a-matic Machine."

He started to sketch the machine. Then his pencil tip broke. He reached into his backpack for another pencil. His fingers brushed against the wishbone he wished on the day before. He took out the pencil and the wishbone. He placed the wishbone on the desk. Then he drew a stick man on a boat. "Dad,..." Tyler bit his lower lip and fought back the tears, "one day I'll be just like you."

But the large, dark skyline twinkling outside his window reminded him of his place in the world. "Nah, that's a stupid wish. I'm just an orphan. I'll never be able to afford a boat. Maybe I can make another wish."

Tyler held his half of the wishbone up to the skyline outside the window. "I wish to figure out a way to build that machine, so I won't have to spend so much time on these dumb homework assignments anymore."

A breeze broke through the still air and ruffled the notebook papers. Wind chimes rang somewhere in the dark, and a chill rushed down Tyler's spine. He looked out the window, then he looked down. A shiny, blue bike was sitting in the alley below. He was sure it wasn't there earlier when he saw the rat. *Whose is it?* he thought. Then he thought he heard the wind whisper, "Go ride."

Tyler's eyes grew wide. "Who said that?"

"Go ride."

Now he was sure he heard it. "Wow, how cool!" No kid in the orphanage had a bike. This was a treat. Tyler threw on his backpack and started to sneak down the stairs. Suddenly, he stopped. He wasn't sure why, but he felt he should take the photo of his father with him. So he quietly turned around and ran back to get the photo. He slipped the photo into his back pocket and tiptoed down the stairs so no one would hear him and try to stop him.

Once outside he looked around to see if anybody was out there. "Hello? Anyone here? Is this your bike?" No one answered. Without waiting any longer, he jumped on the bike and took off down the street.

Tyler sped through the city, weaving in and out of the high rises on the bike. He twisted and turned past coffee shops and newspaper stands. It must have been a magic bike because it went much faster than Tyler was pedaling. "Weeeeeeee! Whoooooa!"

Several minutes went by, as Tyler enjoyed the most exciting bike ride of his life. Then, without warning, the bike came to a screeching halt in front of the silver rotating door of a gigantic skyscraper. Tyler was nearly launched over the handle bars. He jumped off the bike and stood in awe of the tall steel building towering over him. It must have been one hundred stories high. Its glass windows stretched those one hundred stories to a red beacon shining into the dark sky. It wasn't that he had never seen a tall building like this before—in fact, he had seen many everyday of his life as he walked to school from his orphanage; but at night they looked dressed up, larger than life, as if they were dressed in tuxedos headed for a party.

Tyler stepped into a slowly spinning rotating door at the front entrance of the building. Just as he did this, the door picked up speed. Soon it was spinning so fast that Tyler had to grab hold of the railing to keep from flying out. Outside, the world turned into a cloudy blur, and Tyler felt like he was tumbling in a breaking ocean wave.

In the haze, Tyler thought he caught a glimpse of a boat tossing in a stormy sea. Someone was at the helm, but he couldn't get a clear vision of who it was.

A strange deep voice broke his concentration, "Hello, my child."

"Uh, hello? Who is that? What's happening?"

"Don't be afraid, my child. I'm here to help you."

"Help me? Help me with what?"

"I want to guide you—to let you know how you can realize your dream to own a boat and travel around the world seeing different cultures."

"Um, I think you have the wrong kid," Tyler said. "I'm just an orphan. I have no money to buy a boat and travel around the world."

"Tyler, do you know what an entrepreneur is?"

"An ahn-tray-prennnnn-no?"

The voice laughed softly, then said the word again slowly, "An entrepreneur."

"No, what's that?"

"An entrepreneur is a person who starts a business from scratch. Entrepreneurs are the best at making their dreams come true."

"Really, if entrepreneurs are the best at making their dreams come true, then I want to be one! Then I'll be able to own a boat and sail around the world, right?"

"That's right, Tyler, but it's not that easy to be an entrepreneur. It takes a lot of confidence, organization, hard work and dedication. You have to be resourceful and imaginative. Not everyone is cut out to be an entrepreneur.

"That's a lot of big words you are saying, Mister. Who are you?"

"I'm the Great Spirit of the Entrepreneurs. I have come from the land of Profits. You can call me Soté. How badly do you want to become this sea captain?"

"So much I would do ANYTHING for it!"

"Anything?"

"Yes, anything."

"Would you learn to be confident?"

"Yes, I'll learn to be confident."

"Would you learn to be organized?"

"Yes, I'll learn to be organized."

"Would you work hard and never give up?"

"Yes, I'll work hard and never give up."

"OK. Then listen closely, my child. Your dream awaits you at the top of this one-hundred-story building. You must reach the top before sunrise."

"That's no problem. I'll take the elevator."

Soté chuckled. "It's not that easy. This building is unique. Elevators don't go straight to the top. They stop on special floors. When they do, your job is to get off and find the key to the other elevators hidden on the floor. Don't bother looking for stairwells. They will be locked.

"What if there's a fire?"

"If there is a fire, then the stairwells will automatically be unlocked. But only if there is a fire. Now go find your way to the library where your journey begins. If you do not find your way to the top before sunrise, then you will not become an entrepreneur and your dream will not come true; so do not lose sight of time."

"Be very, very careful on your journey. These special floors are not meant for boys like you," warned the Spirit. You may meet beings who wish to stop you from reaching the top. You must be smart. Do not let them get to you.

"Remember, you are not alone. Even though you cannot see me, I'll be guiding you along the way. Now go, my child. You must hurry. It's six o'clock. Sunrise is only twelve and a half hours away."

CHAPTER 2:
CREATIVE JUICE SMOOTHIES

Just then, the revolving doors stopped, and Tyler stood in a beautiful lobby with large columns extending to the ceiling as far as the eye could see. Glass windows surrounded a shiny, white marble tile floor. Huge chandeliers hung from the ceiling. This building was a big place for important people. Tyler could tell that much. Straight ahead was a man standing behind a tall desk. Behind the man, a sign that read "DREAMS COME TRUE" hung on the wall.

"Hello, Tyler. We've been expecting you," the man called from across the lobby.

Tyler approached slowly. The sound of his heels hitting the marble tile echoed off the dark windows. *Click. Click. Click.*

"My name is Mr. Tipmee. I have a note for you, Tyler." Tyler stared at the yellow paper in Mr. Tipmee's hand. "Go on, take it." Mr. Tipmee rattled the paper at Tyler.

Tyler raised his trembling hand to take the paper. The note read:

In the box that rises to the pents,
Stands ancient wood where ideas commence.

Drink from the goblets, creative juice smoothies.
Of them, beware, you must be choosy:

Berries of blue; berries of boysen;
But one of them bares berries of poison.

"Am I suppose to know what this means, Mr. Tipmee?"

"You're supposed to figure it out."

"But it doesn't make any sense."

"Hmmm. Maybe Soté was wrong about you. He sure seemed confident that you were the one. Maybe you're not cut out to be an entrepreneur after all." Mr. Tipmee took the yellow paper from Tyler.

"I am, too, Mr. Tipmee. Give that riddle back. I can do it. You just watch."

Tyler snatched the riddle back and stormed over to a marble bench in the middle of the lobby.

Up by the boxes that rise to the pents.
Pents? What are pents? Tyler paused, then
shrugged and read the next line.

Stands ancient wood where ideas
commence. OK, ancient wood where ideas
commence. Ancient wood. That wall
behind Mr. Tipmee's station is made of
wood. Tyler walked over to the wood wall
near Mr. Tipmee, who was standing there
with his arms crossed.

"Is this wood ancient?"

"Not that I know of."

Not discouraged, Tyler turned the
corner of the wood wall to see two rows of
five elevators each. Each elevator was separated by twisted miniature trees. *Elevators.*
Boxes that rise. Yes, that's it. To the pents?
Each elevator had a set of numbers above it.
"1-10" was etched in stone, above the first on
his left. "11-20" on the next. "21-30", and so
on, up to 100. *Pents? Pentagon? A pent-*
agon is a shape that has five sides, so maybe
it's the elevator that goes to the fifth floor
He pushed the button by the elevator beside
him that read "1-10". Ding. The doors
opened. He walked in, but there were no
buttons. "Yeah, that's helpful," Tyler jumped
off the elevator.

"What did you say, son?"

"Oh, nothing, Mr. Tipmee, just thinking out loud." To himself, he thought, *Now what? Wait a minute, usually buildings have penthouses on the top floor. Maybe "pents" means the penthouse, the top floor. Let's see...,* Tyler looked again at all the numbers. *That would be the one with "91-100" above it.* The dial above the door pointed to "100", indicating the elevator must be on the 100th floor. He pushed the button, and the dial counted down "99, 98, 97, 96..." until it finally reached "1". Ding.

The doors opened. He saw a beautifully polished antique table against the back of the elevator car. Images of butterflies and caterpillars were carved on the drawers. A white lace cloth covered the table.

Tyler ran his hand over the smooth polished edge of the table. Tyler's orphanage didn't have furniture this nice. He knew this table must be from a foreign land, like one of those he'd like to visit by boat someday. Three glass goblets trimmed with gold sat on the table. "So this must be the ancient wood and the goblets of creative juice smoothies."

Tyler picked up the first goblet and held it to the light. The juice was purple. The juice in the second goblet was sapphire blue. The third was nuclear green. Feeling a little thirsty, he started to drink the green one, but before he took a swig, he read the riddle again: *Drink from the goblets, creative juice smoothies. Of them, beware, you must be choosy. Berries of blue, berries of boysen, but one of them bares berries of poison.*

"The blue one must be blueberries. It even smells like blueberries. Boysenberries are purple, and they, too, smell like berries. That leaves the nuclear green one." He smelled it, "Ugh. This stinks! Pewwwwwww-wee! I think this must be the one made of 'berries of poison.'" Tyler poured the green smoothie into the pot of a miniature

tree outside the elevator. Since blue was his favorite color, he chose the blue smoothie, took a deep breath, and without further hesitation, drank every last drop.

A breeze blew through the elevator car, and the doors of the elevator slammed shut; but it was what Tyler saw just before the elevator doors closed, that sent a chill rushing through his body. The tree where he had poured the green smoothie was DEAD!

CHAPTER 3:
THE LIBRARY OF KNOWLEDGE & THE SEEDS OF DOUBT

As Tyler felt the elevator rise, thoughts became remarkably clear. He closed his eyes and thought of his Solve-a-matic Machine. He saw how to design it, how to build it, and every detail of the final product. He thought it would be good to make many of them, so other kids could buy them from him. He could charge a little more than it cost him and make money. He would use that money to buy his boat.

The elevator doors opened to a room shaped like a stop sign with seven lofty walls and an arched doorway. Tyler peered into the room. Oak bookshelves, packed with books, aligned six of the seven walls. In the wall directly facing the arched doorway, stood a gray stone fireplace with a blazing fire.

In the middle of the room, two thick wooden tables rested on a large rug. Opened books and stacks of closed books covered one table. The fire's blaze illuminated a closed laptop computer in the middle of the books. On top of the laptop was a small white envelope. In the center of the other table, pencils, erasers, and papers were neatly stacked.

From the ceiling hung a chandelier of candles. It was too large for the small room. Cobwebs filled the gaps between the candles. The fire snapped and popped. Shadows from the fire and the candles danced about the dimly lit room.

Beyond the chandelier, the ceiling from far away appeared to be covered wall-to-wall in hamburger buns. "Hamburger buns?" Tyler blurted out a little louder than he had intended, "What are those doing on the ceiling?"

Tyler was not sure what to do, so he flipped through a few books on the table. The titles sounded really boring:

Real Estate Law: A Reference
Start Your Own Business
Negotiating With Unions Effectively
Accounting 101

Each book was over six hundred pages long. They were thick, heavy, and terribly intimidating.

"All right, Tyler," Tyler said to himself, "you can do this. I pledge to not give up, no matter what lies ahead."

"You promise?" a voice from behind answered.

"I promi—who said that?" Tyler spun around searching for the source of the voice.

"I did." High on a wooden ladder near the top of a bookshelf was a striking young girl, who looked about ten years old. She had long, thin arms and her dainty hands held her to the ladder. Her sun-bleached hair was thick and pulled back into a ponytail. A cobweb rested right on top of her head. She wore a white shirt and a jean skirt.

"Uh, hello," said Tyler.

The girl climbed down the ladder and extended her hand to shake his, "Hi, I'm Giselle."

"Tyler."

"I know. I've been expecting you."

"Does everybody in the building know I'm here? Everyone keeps saying they are expecting me."

"Who else?"

"Mr. Tipmee, downstairs."

"And?"

"That's all."

"I hardly think that two people should count as 'everyone', do you?"

"I guess not. If you know who I am, then you must know what I'm doing here."

"I do. You're here to become an entrepreneur, aren't you?"

"Yeah, how did you know? Is that why you're here?"

"No, I've seen many of my mother's friends pass through here, but you are the first boy about my age to come."

"Did Soté bring you here also?"

"Soté? No, my mother designed this building." She paused not knowing if she should continue, then submitted, "And she owns it, too. My family lives on one of the floors of this building. My mother home schools me. I'm here working on a book report she's making me do."

"Then, is Soté your father?"

"No. Soté is a spirit who is a friend of my mother's and happens to also rent some floors on this building from my mom. Now step over here, please, Tyler," Giselle pointed to the envelope lying on top of the laptop. "I believe this is addressed to you."

Tyler picked up the envelope. Indeed, it was addressed to Tyler. It read, "Tyler, enclosed is something for you to borrow for your journey. You will have to return it at the end of your journey. But if things go right, that should be no problem for you. – Soté" Tyler opened the envelope and found a hundred one hundred dollar bills. "Wow! Look at all this cash! I'm rich!"

Giselle shook her head. "It's for you to borrow, not to keep. Don't waste it. However, this laptop," Giselle pointed to the laptop, "This is yours to keep."

"To keep?"

"Yes, it's a gift."

"From whom?"

"Soté. It has wireless technology. You will be able to connect to the Internet from anywhere in the building.

"Cool!" Tyler opened the laptop.

"Do you see this small picture of an envelope at the bottom of the screen?" Giselle asked.

"Yeah."

"That means you have unread e-mail." The e-mail read:

Tyler,

Remember, on each floor you must find a key to the elevator that will take you to the next floor. On each floor you visit, you will be given a riddle like the one you received from Mr. Tipmee earlier. There's another one at the end of this letter. These riddles will guide you to the keys. The Internet can also be a great resource for finding the keys. Don't forget, you must make it to the top by sunrise (6:23 A.M.), or your dream will not come true.

Good luck!
Soté

P.S.
Draw your machine.
Tell what it's about,
But beware the sesame seeds of doubt.

Tyler tilted his head towards Giselle, raised his worried eyebrows, and bit his lip. "There's just one little problem."

Giselle saw his eyes drop to the floor. Tyler loved building model sailboats; he was quite skilled at it. Other children at the orphanage liked them so much they would even barter for them; but drawing his Solve-a-matic Machine, now that required an entirely different set of skills. "I can't draw," Tyler confessed.

Not knowing how to respond, she stood silent for a moment, which seemed like an eternity. Then, it hit Giselle, "Well, you're in luck, Tyler."

"I am?"

"Yes, because I draw."

"You do? Awesome!" Tyler's face lit up, "I'll describe the machine, and you can draw it."

Tyler described his machine to Giselle, while she sat at the table and he sprawled out on the floor by the fire with his hands behind his head. She followed his directions carefully, sketching while he dictated. After a few minutes, they took a break to review the drawing.

"No, no, that's all wrong," Tyler said in despair. I said the driving gear should be in the back of the machine, not the front. The pulley is supposed to be at the top. Oh, this is never going to work."

Blip. Tyler felt the lightest touch on his shoulder, as if a moth fluttered by. Without taking his eyes off the sketch, he brushed something from his shoulder.

"I can fix it," Giselle said.

"I don't know. It's hard trying to describe where everything should go. I just don't see how this is going to work. I'm not sure this machine is even useful."

Blip. Blip. Tyler brushed something off his other shoulder.

"Why don't you share the chair with me, Tyler. Maybe it would be easier if you saw what I was drawing."

"OK. Good idea."

Tyler and Giselle resumed the drawing. A few minutes later, "Wait, wait." Tyler grabbed the top of Giselle's pencil. "Not there."

"I know, Tyler. You haven't even seen what I was going to draw."

"I didn't have to see. I knew what you were going to draw. You were going to sketch a knot in the rope, but there's not supposed to be a knot in the rope at that point."

"Well, then that is proof that you should practice some patience, because you see, there was never going to be a knot in the rope. That was a hook for the latch."

"That doesn't look like a hook."

"It doesn't yet because you didn't let me finish."

"Ugh, this is exhausting, Giselle. If this is how it's going to be, then we're never going to finish. I don't have a lot of time to waste.

This is hard. I'm not even sure how the machine should look. How then can I possibly describe it correctly to you?"

Blip. Blip. Blip. Blip. This time Tyler could not ignore the pestering mini-pellets bouncing off his shoulders, his back, his head, and the drawing. They hit the drafting table, soared a foot into the air, then hit the floor.

Giselle bent down to the floor to examine a pellet. She gasped, "Oh no, Tyler. They look like sesame seeds. They are falling from those hamburger buns on the ceiling. They are the sesame seeds of doubt the riddle warned you about."

Just as she said that, it began raining millions of them. The floor, the drawing, and Giselle and Tyler's hair were all covered. One bounced in Tyler's eye, "I can't see." He fumbled around and fell face first into the pile of seeds.

Giselle tried to steal a glance at the ceiling, but had to look away, "Boy, those hamburger buns are loaded with sesame seeds."

"Tyler."

"What?"

"I didn't say anything," Giselle said while she shielded her eyes from the storm.

"If you didn't say anything, then who just called my name?"

"Tyler, it's Soté."

"Soté, help! Where are you?"

"Tyler, you must remain confident. Do not doubt your drawing. Do not doubt your machine."

"Confidence? You mean I need to believe in myself?"

"Yes, and your Solve-a-matic Machine." Soté's voice echoed over again as it faded away.

"How am I suppose to do that when I can't draw?" Blip.

"Soté?" Silence.

"He's gone."

Tyler sat down at the table, brushed a pile of seeds away from the paper, and continued the drawing where Giselle had left off. The raining sesame seeds reduced to a sprinkle and finally stopped altogether. After five minutes, he pushed back from the table, "Done. Perfect."

"Now that you're done drawing the machine, where do you suppose the key is?"

"Open Sesame," Tyler blurted out.

Nothing happened.

"What did you say that for?" asked Giselle.

"Ali Baba in the book *The Thousand and One Nights* used that phrase to open a treasure cave of forty thieves. I thought I'd give it a shot."

"Nice try, but it looks like you'll have to try something else."

"Where's the service elevator?"

"It's behind that fireplace, but I never use that one. I always use the elevator you just used. I've seen this sort of thing in the movies, though. Isn't there usually a fake book somewhere that, when pulled out, makes the fireplace spin around?" Giselle and Tyler looked across the room and up the walls. Where among the tens of thousands of books was the lever for the elevator access?

"There has to be an easier way. Are the books in any kind of order?" Tyler brushed the dust off a nearby book cover.

"Yes, they're in order by authors' names."

"Wait a minute. There's a key next to the fireplace." A brass key stuck out from the stone hearth. Tyler turned it, but nothing happened. He turned it back, still nothing. He took it out and put it back in. Still nothing happened.

Giselle took the key from him and held it towards the firelight. "It's engraved with 'F1.' I wonder what that means. Fire 1?"

"Maybe it's a name of a book. Let me check the Internet for a book named *F1*." Tyler typed 'F1' in the search engine. No matches were found. Just as he was about to shut the lid on the laptop he noticed a key in the upper left area of the keyboard with "F1" on it. He pushed it to see what would happen. The computer's help window popped up on the screen. In the body of the window were the words:

A. Rand

"Did you find something."

"I think I know the author we're looking for."

"Who?"

"A. Rand. See if you can find it."

Giselle moved the ladder to the shelf near the fireplace and climbed up several steps. She leaned way out to the right and reached for a book with "A. Rand" as the author. The fireplace began to shake and rumble. Echoes of Tyler's own voice rang throughout the room:

Oh, this is never going to work.
I dont know. It's hard trying to describe where everything should go. I just don't see how this is going to work.
I'm not sure this machine is even useful.
If this is how it's going to be, we're never going to finish...we're never going to finish...we're never going to finish.

Tyler shouted back at his own voice, "It will work! It is useful! We did finish!" The fireplace spun around to expose a foyer with an elevator.

"Yea!" they cheered.

"Don't forget your plans and your laptop," Giselle reminded Tyler as he jumped on the elevator.

Tyler scrambled to get his plans and the laptop and stuffed them in his backpack. "Aren't you coming?"

"You want me to come?" Giselle looked surprised.

"Sure, come on."

Giselle's book report would have to wait. She jumped on the elevator with Tyler and away they went.

"Ding," the computer rang from inside the backpack.

"Sounds like I have e-mail," Tyler said.

CHAPTER 4:
THE MEDINA

Now you must find the supplies you need,
To build your machine; it takes many
indeed;

The medina has many goods to reap,
But stories trade shopping for sleep.

If you choose to linger too long,
Dreamy notes will seep from the charmer's
song.

Tyler checked his laptop clock. It was 7:50 P.M. Beyond the elevator doors was a orange clay wall with an arched doorway and budding rose bushes on each side. A sign above said, "Medina of Marrakech: The World's Largest Outdoor Market."

Tyler and Giselle peered through the archway into a huge open courtyard surrounded by shops with walls made of that same orange clay. They could hear the rhythmic beat of drums. Inside the courtyard, they could see the shadows of men dressed in robes gathered around dancers, drummers, and snake charmers. Brightly lit merchant booths marked the center of the crowded courtyard. Gray smoke carrying the scent of spices, grilled meats, and toasty flatbreads floated from these booths past Tyler and Giselle, and then rose up into the exotic night sky.

Giselle said, "You need to make a list of the supplies you need."

"Yeah, you're right. I do," Tyler took out his laptop and started typing...

> 20 sheets of Leather
> 20 Corks
> 200 centimeters of Wire
> 250 centimeters of a Garden Hose
> 10 pinches of Cumin Seeds
> …

"Hi."

Tyler stopped typing his list and looked up to see a boy about his age. The boy had a round face, light brown spiky hair, and small cheerful eyes. He wore jeans and a shirt that said, "Z - X."

"Uh. Hello," Tyler said hesitantly, not knowing what the boy wanted.

"Hi, I'm Why Zakracker. You may call me Why."

Tyler scrunched his forehead, "I don't know, you tell me? Why may I call you?"

"Why, don't you know? I just told you."

"Huh?"

Why Zakracker grabbed his stomach and buckled over with laughter, "Get it? My name is 'Why' and you thought I was asking you why you may call me. Ha ha ha!"

Tyler laughed. "That was good. You fooled me. I'm Tyler, by the way," Tyler extended his hand for a handshake.

The boy returned the shake and looked at the laptop resting on Tyler legs. "So, what are you doing? I come to this courtyard all the time, but I've never seen anyone out here with a laptop before."

Tyler explained his task to Why. Why replied, "Oh, I can help you find those supplies. I know this place inside and out."

"Really, you'll help me?"

"Sure, but first I must get some hot mint tea. The tea clears my mind, helps me focus. Have you ever had it?

"No, our tea at the orphanage is cold and sweet. It doesn't taste like mint."

"Oh, it's delicious. Come with me."

Tyler followed Why toward a cluster of merchant booths. Giselle stayed behind double-checking the supply list.

Why was a joke teller. He loved to make people laugh. He and Tyler sat down on the pavement. Why told his jokes, and Tyler listened. Tyler attempted a few jokes himself, but they weren't as funny. Mostly he just laughed at Why's. Soon others joined them to listen and laugh, and before long men from the market surrounded them. They stopped to hear Why tell his jokes. He went on for a long time telling jokes. One could hear the roar of their laughter from miles away. Even a few of the merchants took breaks from their work to join in all the fun.

Meanwhile, Giselle stood outside the huddle, worried. Time was ticking away, and Tyler hadn't even started buying the supplies he needed.

Suddenly, Giselle heard strange music. It was coming from a snake charmer playing his flute. The snake rose out of the basket and danced to the notes. *If you choose to linger too long, Dreamy notes will seep from the charmer's song...*

Oh, no, Giselle plugged her ears, *it's the snake charmer's song the riddle warned us about.*

She pushed through the crowd to warn Tyler, but it was too late. Tyler and Why were both in a deep sleep.

While Tyler slept, Giselle walked through the maze of merchants searching for cork, leather, and wire. She passed booths of artisans carving designs in leather satchels; she passed booths of carpenters assembling wood boxes with camel bone designs; she passed merchants selling sheep's brains. *An interesting assortment of goods they have here.*

After she had collected a few items and had found a small abandoned cart to store them in, she returned to Tyler where he was just beginning to wake up. "Tyler get up! It's 9:15. You have to finish getting your supplies and find the key to the elevator."

Rubbing his eyes, "It's 9:15 already?"

"Yes!" Giselle barked, "You've been telling jokes and sleeping."

"Sleeping?"

"Yes, sleeping. The snake charmer played his song and filled your ears with poisonous notes. Meanwhile, I've been able to find a few supplies for you, but there are still a lot more to get. If we're going to make it before sunrise, then we need to split the list into two. I'll take one; you take the other."

"Whoa, easy now. Take a breath, Giselle." Tyler stood up, brushed the dust off his knees, and looked at his list. It was a long list. "OK, good plan." He and Giselle split the list as she suggested.

After half an hour, Tyler had found all his supplies except rope and some boards of wood. He pushed the cart up and down the rows of merchants, stopping at some along the way. He stopped to ask a camel breeder if he knew where he could get some rope. The breeder sent him in the direction of the hammock maker. Tyler was getting tired so he sat on a street bench.

A robed figure, whose face was hidden in the shadow of his hood, walked briskly towards Tyler. He didn't look like he was going to slow down. Tyler thought he might plow straight into him, knocking him and the bench to the ground. He was trying to decide whether to jump left or right to get out of his way, when the figure leaned down and whispered in his ear, "Webs lead to ancient labyrinths." Before Tyler could respond, the figure scurried out of sight into the dark crowd.

"Webs lead to ancient labyrinths, hmmmm. What did he mean by that?"

"I'm done." Giselle plopped down beside Tyler on the bench. "Are you?"

"No, not yet."

Suddenly, Why Zacracker appeared and wedged his way in between the two benchwarmers, "Howdy."

"Oh, no. Not you again," Tyler laughed. "Don't tell me anymore jokes!" He plugged his ears.

"I'm happy to see you, too, Tyler."

"You guys, the strangest thing just happened to me," Tyler said, and he proceeded to tell them about the mystery man's message: *Webs lead to ancient labyrinths.*

"Let me check something." Why reached for Tyler's laptop.

After typing and studying the screen for what seemed like forever to Tyler, Why finally said, "That's what I thought." Why pushed the laptop over to Tyler.

"He was referring to the World Wide Web—the Internet—when he said 'webs'. Also, beyond the outer ring of this courtyard is a maze of narrow passageways with small wooden doorways all along the way. These doorways don't look like much, but behind some of them are beautiful homes we call riads. The maze of narrow passageways is your labyrinth."

"On the Internet, I found a map of this medina and the maze of passageways that wind between the courtyard and the medina wall. Follow me." Not waiting for Tyler and Giselle, Why took off for the edge of the medina. Tyler stuffed the laptop in his backpack, Giselle grabbed the cart, and they both ran after Why.

Why led Tyler and Giselle through an arched opening. The narrow cobblestone path twisted and turned. Not too far into the maze, Tyler and Giselle lost all sense of direction.

"We hardly know this guy, Tyler. What if he's leading us into a trap? After all, he did distract you with his jokes. How do you know that wasn't on purpose?" whispered Giselle.

"It's not a trap. Why wouldn't do that. He's our friend."

"He said behind *some* doorways are beautiful homes," Giselle added as they walked past a beaten looking door, "What do you think lies behind the other doors?"

Why stopped in front of a small door at the end of a dead-end path. Hanging from the door was a Scorpion door knocker. "Behold, the home of the lumberjack Scorpio and his wife, Rita, the rope maker."

Scorpio was a small Arab man in a plaid robe. He welcomed them with a nod. There was something friendly in his toothless smile and beady eyes.

Scorpio led them past a small courtyard in the front of their home. Pillows in beautiful tapestries and candles in glass lanterns were arranged neatly in groups on the floor. A fountain full of floating red rose petals marked the center of the room.

Beyond the courtyard past some arches and columns, was Scorpio's shop, filled with wood boards and hanging ropes of various sizes. Tyler found the wood and rope he needed to complete his set of supplies and walked over to Scorpio's desk to make his purchases.

"Take a look." Scorpio handed Tyler a leather satchel with intricate decorative cut-outs. Tyler admired the designs.

"Handmade," Scorpio read Tyler's mind, "Beautiful, no?"

"Yes, it's amazing."

"You want? Nothing like it in the world. Only made here. I make you deal."

Tyler purchased the little leather satchel along with the wood and the rope. After saying their goodbyes to Why, Tyler turned to Giselle, "See? It helps to take time to make friends. Why really helped us out."

Raising her eyebrows Giselle added, "Yeah, but you took a little too long. It almost cost you your entrepreneurship."

But Tyler was right, and he *had* learned a valuable lesson. It helps to make friends. You never know when a friend might turn out to be a life-saver one day. In the spirit of his new-found lesson, he decided he better show his appreciation for his other new friend. Once they were back out in the courtyard, he took the satchel out of his bag and handed it to Giselle.

"For you. Thanks for bailing me out."

Giselle examined the little leather satchel with pretty carvings etched on it. To her surprise, she found an elevator key inside it. "Hey, look what I found!" she shouted as she showed Tyler the key.

"Yes!"

"Rock on!"

They tried the key out on every door they passed, until finally, on their tenth try, they found the elevator.

CHAPTER 5:
TIME TO MARKET

On the ride to the next floor, Tyler received another e-mail. It read:

```
Build your machine, then put it to test,
Be sure to take breaks to rest;

Take your time, but not too much,
Finish before the opposite of lunch;

Than Sam the Spider, you must be faster,
Or your machine will give way to disaster.
```

"Finish at the opposite of lunch? What do you suppose that means?" asked Giselle.
"Well, it might mean breakfast or supper."

"But neither of those are really opposites of lunch, just alternatives."

"Yeah, hmmmm. Oh wait, it's 10:00 P.M. now, so I bet 'the opposite of lunch' must be referring to time. The time of lunch is noon."

"...and the opposite of noon is midnight!" Giselle added.

Tyler fumbled in his pocket. The picture of his father wasn't there anymore! He must have dropped it somewhere. "Oh no."

"What?"

"I think I've lost something."

"What did you lose?"

"Just something very special to me."

"Do you want to retrace our steps to look for it?"

Tyler hesitated. "No, no. We don't have time." A tear welled up in his eye, but he wiped it away before Giselle could see it.

Right then the elevator door sprung open. Before them was a ramp leading down into a small concrete room. To the left of the room was a wall of closed garage doors. In the center of the room stood a mechanic's orange, metal tool chest. A saw, a drill, and many other workshop tools hung on the wall to the right. Hanging on the brick wall straight ahead was a large clock as tall as Tyler himself.

A large black spider stood on a platform high above them. He did not speak to them; he refused to look at them, but Giselle and Tyler both knew he must be "*Sam the Spider*" mentioned in the riddle. Sam the Spider shoveled large rocks the size of soccer balls, shredded paper, and what looked like metal scissors into a large funnel bolted to the ceiling above them. The bot-

tom of the funnel was closed off by a small plate which kept the mixture of rocks, papers, and scissors from spilling out all over Giselle, Tyler, and their work area. A metal rod ran the length of the room, connecting the plate to a tiny lever on the clock. The lever was arranged in just a way that when the hour hand struck 12:00, it would make contact with the lever. The small movement it would cause would be just enough to shift the rod and move the plate under the funnel. This would cause the rocks, paper, and scissors to spill all over their work area and destroy everything.

"I'll get to work assembling the Solve-a-matic Machine," Tyler pushed the cart out of the elevator and headed down the ramp towards the mechanic's tool chest and the work area. He examined an electric screwdriver. Then, he looked at his supplies piled high in the cart. He frowned. "Ugh, how am I to make heads from tails of this? What a mess!" The pile towered over him like a big dinosaur. Should he start with constructing the pulley system? Or should he start with soldering the metal together? Or would it make most sense to begin with wiring the electronics. Tyler stared at the pile-o-saurus and scratched his head.

Tyler decided to start with soldering the metal for the machine, but then couldn't find the solder. Then he decided to start building the pulley system, but he couldn't find the rope. Then, he decided to build the electronic piece, but he couldn't find the wires. The ticking of the large clock overhead grew louder, and as it did, his mind grew fuzzy; the room started to spin.

Soté's voice whispered in Tyler's ear, "Take a break. Sometimes it's better to stop and rest, so you can start again fresh, than to burn yourself out with continuous work." Tyler closed his eyes for a few minutes and tried to clear his mind.

One minute passed.

Five minutes passed.

Ten minutes and the clouds in Tyler head began to part. He had an idea—*I'll sort the pile first.*

Checking the clock on the wall, Tyler exclaimed, "11:05 P.M.! Yikes! We have less than an hour. We have to get cracking."

"We?" Giselle smiled.

"Oh, sorry, Giselle. Will you, please, help me sort this pile, so we can build this machine?"

"Since you asked nicely, then yes, I can help you."

Together Giselle and Tyler worked to build the machine. A few minutes later, Tyler had an idea, "Wouldn't it be great to have the machine celebrate when it spits out the finished homework assignment?"

"Celebrate? How so?" asked Giselle.

"Well, I was thinking I would build it so that when the homework was just about to spit out, the lights will start flashing and the machine will make repeating 'ding-ding, ding-ding' sounds."

"Cool. Do you know how to do that?"

"Yes, but it's going to take half an hour at least."

"Don't you need that time to test the machine, to make sure it's working properly."

"Yeah, but maybe I can shorten some of the testing time."

"Tyler, I think maybe you should focus these last minutes on testing the machine. It just needs to work. That will be more than enough for the kids out there looking for an easier way to get their homework done. If it doesn't work properly, then the kids will spread the word that your machine is just junk. You don't want that, do you?"

"No, not at all. I guess you're right, Giselle. I'll save the celebration feature for a later, improved version of the Solve-a-matic Machine."

Tyler ran his last test on the Solve-a-matic Machine. The homework was just right. They drew in a deep breath and exhaled with a huge hug.

"You did it," Giselle said.

"We did it," Tyler corrected her.

The clock above showed 11:56 P.M. The doors on the face of the clock opened and out popped a mechanical cuckoo bird. "Cuckoo, cuckoo," it said. As it did, a key fell from its mouth down to the floor.

"The key! Yea!" They jumped up and down.

"Let's go!" Tyler cried out with joy.

On the wall by the garage doors, they found a key socket. When they tried out the key, the garage doors rattled open. "Come on." Tyler and Giselle loaded the Solve-a-matic Machine into the cart and then rested the blueprints on top. They pushed it towards the garage doors. Behind the garage doors was an elevator standing wide-open. They jumped on. From inside Tyler's backpack, the laptop chimed.

"Sounds like I have another e-mail."

CHAPTER 6:
PIRATE PARROTS

```
Beware pirate parrots who'll steal your plans;
Pat on your nose, if you can;

Plans in hand, you won't see Giselle,
But do not fret, you'll find her well.
```

When the elevators opened, the smell of rain rushed in. Giselle and Tyler stepped off into a dark, damp forest. The moon was the only source of light. The thick trees rose to the sky. Their rain-soaked leaves, the size of small cars, blocked the moonlight from the damp, soft forest floor.

A bright green, wide-eyed tree frog sat motionless on a rock beside one of the trees. He stared intently at Tyler and Giselle. The air was humid. Giselle's hair frizzed within seconds of stepping off the elevator, giving her witch-like hair. The frog's eyes popped out in fear at the sight of her. Then he quickly hopped away into the forest shadows.

"This place is wild." Tyler strapped on the backpack that held his laptop.

"This place is wild," a strange nasal voice echoed from above.

"Who's there?"

"Who's there," echoed the voice. A parrot with an eye-patch swooped down from the tree above and swiped Tyler's blueprints right off the cart.

"My plans! Giselle, he has my plans!"

"My plans! Giselle, he has my plans," the parrot repeated as he flew off between the trees.

Tyler took off running after the parrot. He ran, but the parrot disappeared in the darkness. Tyler stopped to listen. Crickets chirped, frogs croaked, and water dripped, but no sign of the parrot. *What's that rhythmic sound? It sounds familiar, almost* mechanical, but like nothing I would expect to hear in a jungle. Tyler crouched down and peered around a large jungle leaf looking in the direction of the sound.

"Kanku, the machine is jammed again," Tyler heard one parrot squawk to another.

"All right, I'll be there in a minute."

A team of five parrots all wearing bandanas on their head were running copy machines. Tyler, frustrated, looked to his riddle for help. *Pat on your nose, if you can.* Tyler patted his nose, but nothing happened. Deciding to charge in and take his plans back with sheer force, he started to clear a path through the bushes.

"I wouldn't do that if I were you," a voice from behind him said. Tyler whipped around to see a monkey dangling from the tree above, swinging by one arm. His other arm carefully balanced a banana between two fingers and scratched his armpit with the other fingers.

"Those parrots are very dangerous; they have a deadly peck. They'll peck your nose right off your face. See mine?" the monkey pointed to his nostrils. "Gone. They have no mercy. See, a long time ago, a cruel boy with his pet monkey shot BBs at them, and ever since then, they hate all boys and monkeys."

"But they stole my plans for my Solve-a-matic Machine. I need to get them back."

"Forget about the plans. It's too dangerous. They are not worth it."

"I can't forget about them. They are my life's work!"

"Your life's work! Ha! How old are you?"

"Ten."

"Only Ten? You have plenty of time to make another machine. Forget about this one," the monkey said.

"No! I will not. It's my machine. I spent hours working on it, and they have no right to it." Tyler stood up and started walking towards the parrots.

"Wait," whispered the monkey. Tyler stopped without turning back towards the monkey. "If you insist on being stubborn and walking into that deathtrap, then I suggest you, at least, protect yourself. Only then will you have half a chance of making it out of there with your nose still intact."

"How do you suggest I do that?" Tyler turned around.

"I'll tell you if you pick that banana above your head and hand it to me." Above Tyler's head were twenty or so clusters of yellow bananas. He reached up and picked one banana, then handed it to the monkey.

"That's more like it. I'm J.J., by the way."

"Hello, J.J., I'm Tyler."

J.J. walked behind a tree. Unrecognizable objects flew out from the tree and into the shadows. "Just a minute. I know it's here somewhere," J.J. called from behind the tree. More objects flung out from the other side of the tree into the shadows. "Ah ha! Here it is."

J.J. stepped out with an umbrella. "This, my friend, is an umbrella.

"I know what an umbrella is."

"But wait. It's not just any umbrella; it's a patent umbrella."

"Patent? What's that?"

"A patent umbrella will protect you from the pirate parrot's peck. Use it when you go in to take back your plans."

Tyler ran his hand over the umbrella. It was forest green with a cursive gold '*P*' stitched on it. He spun it around a bit. "OK, I'm ready."

"Before you go," J.J. extended his hand to Tyler, "Here's my phone number. Give me a call if you get in another bind like this."

J.J. handed Tyler his business card. "J.J. Junglehammock, Attorney at Law," it said. Tyler thanked him, stuffed the business card in his pocket, and turned back around to face the copy center. Out of Tyler's sight, J.J. raised his clasped hands to his mouth and softly gnawed on a finger, "Good luck, Tyler." The truth was, J.J. wasn't sure if the umbrella still held the magical powers in it. He had had the umbrella for years, and over time the powers might have drained out. Never-the-less, he was nervous for Tyler, but he also realized it was Tyler's only hope to recover his plans.

With the umbrella held high over his head, Tyler charged into the jungle copy center, grabbed the plans, and ran towards the elevators he came from. He turned back to see that no one was chasing him. Stunned, he stopped. *It worked!*

Then he heard the parrots laughing. *What are they laughing at?* Tyler looked down to see that in his hands he held a set of blueprints for a birdhouse. "A birdhouse? Darn it! These aren't my plans."

He stomped back to the copy center, this time swinging the umbrella to move the large leaves from his path. The parrot who had stolen his plans dove at him from a limb above. Tyler swung the umbrella at him and knocked him to the ground. He saw his plans sitting on the copy machine. He snatched them, but another parrot grabbed his pants with his beak.

Tyler kicked him off, then opened the umbrella and spun it in the face of the parrots. He ran out of the rain forest's copy center as fast as he could towards the elevators. This time, all five of the parrots chased after him.

Tyler tripped and fell face down. Spitting the dirt from his mouth, he sat up to see what caused him to fall. It was a small, beautiful wood treasure chest with golden trim. An imprint of an umbrella with a cursive 'P' was carved into the hood. He knelt down and turned the key in the keyhole, but to Tyler's disappointment, the treasure chest did not open.

"Ding." He turned away from the treasure box to see what made that sound. There inside the trunk of a huge tree was an elevator with the doors wide open. The parrots were making a beeline for him. Tyler picked up the beautiful treasure chest and his plans, and he ran inside the elevator. He pushed the button over and over trying to get the door to close.

"Come on, elevator. Close! Close!" It seemed like an eternity waiting for the doors to close. The parrots swooped down. The doors closed catching a wing in their path. The parrot's scream pierced Tyler's ears. Then Tyler flinched as he heard the other parrots plow one by one into the side of the elevator.

Tyler collapsed in exhaustion as the elevator started to rise. He stuffed the beautiful treasure chest into his backpack. "Giselle? Oh no, I left Giselle!" Tyler frantically pushed the down button, but the elevator kept rising.

"Giseeeeeeeeeeeeeeeeeeeeeeeeeeeeelle!"

CHAPTER 7:
REALTY SEA

Tyler decided to check his e-mail while he rested inside the climbing elevator. It read:

Congratulations, you successfully acquired a patent, and your Solve-a-matic Machine has been protected from the pirate parrots. Now it's time to build a factory to mass produce your machine. That means you must first find some land to buy. Find the right land to build your factory, and there will be your key. Find a bad lot, and you'll never see your factory built.

Find a place to produce many
machines;
Use discretion with the eight-
legged queen;

Be cautious of encroaching stones,
Hidden bones,
Restrictive zones;

Avoid the teeth with fins;
Better to deal with dolphins;
Find the right key,
Find your factory.

"Welcome to Realty Sea, Tyler! I've been expecting you." Standing outside the elevator with plump, glossy, red lips and long black eyelashes embracing her bright blue, sparkling eyes stood an octopus. Not a single strand of her blond hair was out of place, and shiny silver bracelets adorned all eight of her arms. "Hello, let me introduce myself. I'm Octopush, your real estate agent. I'm here to help you find the land to build your factory on."

"Can you help me find my friend, Giselle?"

"Your friend? I don't specialize in finding friends. I specialize in finding land, houses, and buildings."

"But she could be in danger," Tyler said. Octopush suggested Tyler use her cell phone to call the police, which he did. The police told him they couldn't do anything until she had been missing for twenty-four hours. But they did take a description of her. Tyler frowned and hung up the phone. The policeman couldn't help him; Octopush couldn't help him. Tyler felt responsible. He had been so caught up in saving his plans that he let her get out of his sight.

Beyond Octopush were hundreds of small islands. *Maybe Giselle was somewhere out on one of those islands*, he thought. Some were rising up out of the sea; others were sinking below the sea. Some appeared to be floating away; others were floating closer. Some were large; some were small. Behind him he saw the same sight—islands as far as the eye could see. In fact, he realized he, too, was standing on an island.

Octopush handed him a list of islands with prices and sizes. Thinking of what he needed to build his factory, Tyler started to eliminate the islands by price and size. He narrowed it down to three.

"Inni-minnie-miney-moe."

Soté's voice whispered with the wind, "Make sure you visit the islands; walk around them; feel their dirt between your fingers; smell their air. Get to know the properties before you buy one."

"You know what, Octopush. I think I'd like to go out and see these islands first before picking one."

"Oh Tyler, that will take a while. Are you sure? I have three other people looking at these islands. If we waste time visiting them, it's likely someone will come along and purchase one out from under your nose."

"Ring, ring." Octopush's cell phone rang. "Just a second, sugar pie. I need to get this."

While Octopush talked on the phone, Tyler thought it over. It was tempting to jump on it. What if someone purchased the perfect island before he could? Then he'd have no place to build his factory. Then what would he do? However, he could not get Soté's words out of his mind, "Make sure you visit the islands, walk them...get to know the properties before you buy one." *I better listen to Soté*, Tyler finally decided.

Octopush hung up the phone. "No, Octopush, I really want to see them before I make a decision. Let's go see them."

"Well alright, if you insist, but I warned you." Tyler and Octopush hopped into the dingy banked on the shore nearby and away to the islands they rowed.

"Welcome to Amphibian Island." Octopush and Tyler jumped out of their dingy onto very wet sand. Amphibian Island was a beautiful island adorned with a clear, pale blue lagoon. Clusters of palm trees danced in the breeze.

A crab came crawling up on the beach with a clipboard in one claw. "You must be Camille the Inspector," Octopush called out to the crab.

"Yes, it's a beautiful island, isn't it?"

"Yes, I love it," Tyler nodded.

"Well, don't get too excited about it," said the crab. "This island is in a flood zone. The whole island will be under water come high tide. Knowing that would be unacceptable for his factory, Octopush and Tyler headed out for the next island on their list.

Tyler stood on the shore of the second island facing Allen the Angel Fish Inspector. Octopush's phone rang. "You guys talk it over. I've got to get this."

"It's a large island. It's plenty big enough to build my factory on, don't you think?" Tyler asked.

"Sure. If you don't mind the eel easement swimming around," warned Inspector Allen.

"The eel easement? What are they?"

"The eel is a snake-shaped fish. There are thousands of them living in colonies right off the shore of this island. The easement gives them the right to swim here."

"What gives them the right to swim here?"

"The easement. An easement is a right held by someone, the eels in this case, to use land belonging to someone else for a specific purpose."

"Yikes, sounds horrific. No way. Thanks for the information, Inspector. Octopush, let's go."

Octopush nodded while still talking on her phone and followed him back out to the dingy.

"Another fabulous island," Tyler said while standing on the shore of the third island. "I'm sure something is wrong with it. Inspector Tess, what do you see? Anything?"

Inspector Tess, a green sea turtle, asked, "What did you say you wanted to do with the property?" She looked at her notes.

"I'm building a factory to mass produce my Solve-a-matic Machine."

"Hmmmmm. Well, I would agree with you that it is a fabulous island—if you were building a house to live in, but not so for a factory. You see, unfortunately this fabulous island has been zoned for residential buildings—homes, duplexes, apartments—places where people live and sleep. It's not for factories.

Octopush's phone rang again.

Tyler and Octopush said goodbye to Tess and headed back to their dingy. Tyler sighed, "It's a good thing I didn't buy any of those three islands just by looking at the list you showed me. Unfortunately, I still have nothing. I'm never going to find the perfect island for my factory." Tyler imagined a big sailboat gliding towards the horizon out of sight with the sun setting down on his dream.

The wind shifted direction, blowing Tyler's hair into his eyes and waking him from his daydream. "Wait, now, suga' pie. Don't give up so soon. Let me pull a new list." Octopush went to the back of the dingy, pushed some buttons on her laptop, and printed a new list from her printer. "Uh-huh–Uh-huh–hmmmm." Octopush's manicured nails ran through the list one by one. All of sudden her face lit up. "Well look at this, suga' pie. A new island has just been placed on the market."

"Placed on the market?" Tyler asked, confused.

"Has just been listed for sale," Octopush explained. "It looks like a perfect match."

"Then let's go check it out."

The newly listed island *was* perfect. It was the right size, had no eel easements, and was zoned for a factory. Tyler had found his land.

Now he needed to borrow some money to pay for the island. There were folks who lent money for just that purpose, but he didn't know where to find them. He asked

Octopush. Sure enough, Octopush knew where to take Tyler to find the lenders – Lender's Island.

"But Tyler, they don't lend money to just anyone who walks up the shore. Do you have a lawyer? You may need some help," said Octopush. Tyler bowed his head and slumped his shoulders. He did not have a lawyer.

Just then he felt the business card in his pocket – the business card J.J. Junglehammock, the monkey, had given him. He pulled it out and reread it. "Attorney at Law," it said in big black letters. Then he replied, "As a matter of fact, Octopush, I DO have a lawyer. May I use your phone?"

So Tyler used Octopush's cell phone to call J.J. Junglehammock. He felt certain J.J. would be able to pull some strings.

When J.J. arrived, he agreed to go with them to Lender's island under one condition. "What's that?"

"You get me some bananas. I don't go out on row boats without a stash of bananas, just in case I get stranded. There's a banana bunch hanging over there." J.J. pointed to a lush banana tree by the shore."

"You want me to go get you the bananas?" asked Tyler.

"Yes."

"Why can't you get them?"

"Because, I just can't."

"That's not a reason."

"Do you want me to go on the dingy with you or not?"

"Oh, all right." Tyler went to pick bananas for J.J.

Tyler, J.J. and Octopush jumped into the dingy and headed to Lender's Island. As they approached the island, they saw a sign, "We lend money." They rowed closer to check it out. Just then, fins popped up out of the water and surrounded the boat. "Oh no! These lenders are sharks! They could tip our boat. Let's get out of here! Row! Row! Faster!"

Tyler and J.J. rowed as fast as they could. The sharks bumped the dingy with forceful blows, one after another. Octopush waved her eight arms in a circle trying to regain her balance and not fall out. Her cell phone fell overboard and a shark jumped up and gobbled it down, nearly taking the sucker cups off Octopush's tentacles. "Ahhhhhhh! My phone, my phone." Octopush started to cry. Tears ran down her cheeks washing away all her make-up.

"Don't cry, Octopush. You can get a new phone when we go ashore."

Octopush wiped away her tears and grabbed an extra oar lying in the dingy and beat back the sharks. Tyler and J.J. continued to row as fast as they could. Finally the sharks, tiring of the game, turned away.

As Tyler rounded the other side of the island, a sign came into view. "Dolphin Bank – we lend money". Remembering the riddle,... *avoid the teeth with fins, better to deal with dolphins...*, he knew this was the place to get his loan.

When the purchase of the island was complete, Tyler said goodbye to J.J. and Octopush, whose new phone was already ringing. Then he rowed out to visit his new island.

He secured the dingy to the shore and walked around, planning where his factory would be built. A sand crab scurried over his bare feet and back behind a dune of sea oats. Out of curiosity Tyler followed the crab. Behind the dune, stood a sandy, old blue wooden sign. He brushed away the years of sand that were encrusted on it. It read, "Welcome to Key Island." *Find the right key, find your factory,* Tyler recalled the riddle. *The key here is not an actual key at all. The island called "Key" is the key!*

Behind him the sound of cranes, tractors, jackhammers and electric saws filled his ears. He turned to see his factory take form. It happened in an instant. Tractors rose out of the sand. Then they morphed into a concrete floor. The trees turned to cranes, which turned to tall brick walls. What was once just an oasis of sand and palm trees, now stood a chic, strong factory, shiny and new. Tyler stared up at his exquisite factory. A sense of accomplishment came over him. He had never been so proud in his life. He now owned a factory.

He walked to the front door of the factory. He tried to open it, but the door sprang back like elevator doors. Indeed it was an elevator.

CHAPTER 8:
TUMBLEWEED DESERT
WINDSTORM

Once on the elevator, Tyler rubbed his eyes and yawned. With all the action going on, he hadn't noticed how tired he was getting. It didn't help that his backpack was loaded with a laptop, the treasure chest, and his blueprints. Carrying all that weight around was also wearing him out. He checked the time on his laptop. *Let's see—it's 2:45 A.M. I didn't realize it was so late.* The elevator continued to rise, so he used this extra time to check the Internet to see what time the sun rises in Nessibus. This morning it was supposed to rise at 6:23 A.M. *Yikes, I have to hurry.* He read his e-mail:

There are four floors left to go. For this floor, you must solve this riddle:

To multiply your machine, you'll need a hand—
Easier done without wind and sand;

Sincerity and incentives can lead to hires,
But force will only set off fires.

While Tyler finished reading the riddle, a gust of hot, dry air hit his face and filled his clothes. He stepped off the elevator and welcomed the hot breeze as the only relief from the brutal sun. Even the cacti, who love a hot, dry climate, seemed a bit wilted in this vast desert.

Isn't it nighttime? What is this world where the sun shines in the middle of the night? he thought. *Could it be that I've stepped out on the other side of Earth where the sun is shining?*

He saw a water well in the distance. *I did not know there were wells in the desert. What kind of place is this?* Just when he thought he had seen it all, he saw the strangest sight of all: one thousand gloved hands tossing about in the desert wind like tumbleweeds. The gloves came in many sizes, and their fabrics varied in color and texture.

About twenty feet ahead of him was a train track with a shiny red train. The track came from around a canyon on his right, and it disappeared into the horizon on his left. Hanging on the outside of the train engine was a rope tied in a circle. The phrase "H.R. Railroad" was written on the car in large black letters.

He decided to check it out. The inside of the train looked like any other passenger train with rows and rows of empty seats, except each seat had a sign hanging on it. One said 'Electrician'; another said 'Assembly Line Manager'; another said 'Bolt Tightener'. *These are the jobs I need to fill to get my factory up and running.*

He peered out the window of the train and remembered the riddle: *To multiply your machine, you'll need a hand, easier done without wind and sand.* He then understood that his mission was to get the tumbling gloves into a seat on the train.

He knew his biggest challenge was to *catch* the tumbling gloves. They wouldn't sit still long enough for him to grab them. As he stepped off the train, he noticed the looped rope again, hanging from the side of the train engine. He decided to use it to lasso the gloves. Now, Tyler had never tried to lasso anything before in his life, so this was going to be a challenge. He started to twirl the lasso over his head. He released the spinning lasso, and aimed it at a tumbleweed glove, but to no avail. He didn't even come close. He noticed smoke rising from the rope resting in the sand. A closer look showed a small fire on the rope. *How did that happen?* he wondered. He hurried to stomp it out.

Then he heard something in the distance. As he walked in the direction of the sound, he determined it came from the water well. "Help!" called a weak voice from the well. That voice sounded familiar, thought Tyler.

"Giselle?"

"Tyler?"

"Giselle, it *is* you! Are you ok?"

"Tyler, help me. I'm down here. I can't get out!"

"Just a sec, Giselle. I'm going to lower a rope down to you." Tyler untied the knot in his rope and threw one end over the crank that suspended over the well. Then he threw the other end down into the well.

Giselle called up, "First, pull up the cart with the machine in it. Then come back and get me."

"The cart? The cart is down there, too?"

"Yes, it's right here."

"Is my Solve-a-matic Machine still in it?"

"Let me check...," Tyler heard some rattling down in the darkness of the well. "Yes, it's here, just like you left it."

"That's a relief. OK, Giselle, hook it up, and I'll raise it," Tyler called down. When Giselle had the cart secure, Tyler turned the crank with all his might. Slowly he raised it up. He pulled the cart out and untied the rope. He quickly inspected his Solve-a-matic

Machine, then transferred the treasure chest and his blueprints from his backpack to the cart. *There, that should make the backpack lighter*, he thought.

Then Tyler lowered the rope back down into the well to retrieve Giselle. He had raised her about halfway up when she called out from the well, "Hurry, Tyler. It hurts to hang on."

"Don't give up, Giselle. I've got you. Just hang on!"

Tyler pulled the crank as hard as he could. He was starting to get tired, and the sun beat down on him mercilessly. Beads of sweat formed on his forehead and upper lip. "Is there any water in this well?"

"No, it's bone dry. Hurry, Tyler, I'm slipping."

Tyler took in a deep breath and gave it all he had for one last crank. Giselle grabbed the well wall and quickly climbed out to safety.

Tyler fell to the ground in utter exhaustion, gasping for breath. After a minute of panting, he was finally able to speak. "What happened in the rain forest, Giselle?" he managed to ask in between breaths.

"In the rain forest, I fell with the cart into a hole. It felt like I fell forever, and then, suddenly, I stopped completely. I was dizzy from falling, but I think I saw a hazy light below me. But that was just for a moment. When the haze lifted, and I no longer felt dizzy, I realized I was looking up at the light, not down. It was as if I had reached the other side of the Earth! The cart sat beside me, just as it looked standing beside me in the forest. It's magic, I tell ya, pure magic."

"That's so weird! I'm just glad I found you," Tyler said. "I was really worried about you." Then they sat quietly for a moment not sure how to take the events that had just happened to them. Giselle looked around at the strange land, then broke the silence, "Did you get a riddle for this place?"

"Yeah." Tyler read the riddle to Giselle and explained his idea to try to lasso the gloves. "The problem is I don't know how to lasso. Right before I found you, I tried it. It isn't as easy as it looks on TV."

"Once? Twice? That's not enough." Giselle looked at her watch. "It's already 3:05 A.M. You have less than four hours left to finish, and you still have three floors to go after this one. So listen to me. I once saw this cattle show on TV..." Giselle went on to describe the lasso technique she had seen on TV.

Inspired, Tyler twirled the lasso over his head again, but he had trouble keeping it twirling. Once he got the hang of it, he tried throwing it out at a tumbleweed glove, but the glove slipped right through the hole in the rope. Again, a small stream of smoke rose from the rope. "It's burning!" yelled Giselle. "Quick, stomp it out!"

Tyler stomped on the rope where the small fire had started.

"Those fires are weakening my rope, and it's the only one I have. Every time I try to lasso a glove, I start a fire."

"You know the riddle says something about using force will start fires. Maybe the lasso isn't the way you should be going about it."

Looking at the gloves tossing about in the wind, Tyler sighed, "How do you suggest I capture them, Giselle? Do you have a better idea?"

"No."

"I've got to learn how to close the rope in mid-air before I can capture a glove. Giselle, will you stand very still and pretend to be a glove?"

"What? No."

"Please, Giselle. You are my only hope."

"Oh, all right."

It took Tyler twenty tries, but he finally figured out how to pull the rope tight in mid-air and tighten it around Giselle's body. But when he tried it on the gloves, the gloves moved too fast. They would slip out of the rope before he could secure it. Each time he missed, another small fire had to be stomped out. His rope was beginning to fall apart.

"Take a break, Tyler. You must be exhausted."

"I am. This is tough." Tyler sat down in the sand, rested his elbows on his knees and lowered his head.

"Tyler, this is Soté."

"Soté? Where are you?"

"I'm here with you, Tyler. I have been watching you struggle. You should talk to the gloves. Look at each carefully and try to see the good in each—the unique talent or attribute that makes one stand out from the others."

"I can do that."

"Give them some incentive for coming to work at your factory. Tell them how much you will pay them."

"I can do that, too." Tyler jumped up with his rope in hand and brushed the sand off his pants. He twirled the rope over his head again. "Don't you want a job, tumbleweed gloves?" Tyler cried out. One glove grabbed on to a nearby cactus. "Don't you want to work at the greatest factory there ever was?" Just as Tyler slung the rope in the direction of the glove, the glove let go of the cactus and tumbled off into the distance. Giselle stomped out the fire this time.

"Be sincere," said Soté's voice, carried by the wind. "Be sincere. They will see through empty promises and false flattery. And don't forget the incentives." As Tyler stood watching the tumbleweed gloves toss about in the wind, Soté's words must have finally clicked in his head, because what happened next was an amazing transformation of events.

"Hey you, the glove made of denim," Tyler called out, "I'm looking for a glove who is strong to put my machines together." The denim glove hovered in front of Tyler. "How about $10 an hour?" The glove turned its back on Tyler and started to tumble away. "That's not enough? OK, how about $20 an hour?" The denim glove stopped and faced Tyler. Then it gave a thumbs-up sign. Tyler roped it and dragged it over. "You are going for a train ride. Welcome aboard."

"Hey, you, the glove in that great shade of green," Tyler called out. The green glove grabbed hold of a cactus. "I need a green thumb to manage my plant, my factory.

You would be perfect. I'll pay you $20 an hour." The green glove reached two fingers inside the glove and pulled out a paper rolled and tied with a blue ribbon. Tyler untied and unrolled the paper. It said:

THE
UNIVERSITY OF NESSIBUS
AWARDS

GREEN GLOVE

A

MASTERS IN
BUSINESS ADMINISTRATION

JUNE 1995

"Oh, you went to college to learn how to be a manager and this is your college degree." The green glove nodded. "I guess that means you want more. How about $30 an hour?"

The glove shook itself back and forth to say, 'No.'

"OK, then how about $40 an hour?"

The green glove gave the thumbs-up sign. $40 an hour was fine with him.

"Hey you, the glove with the long fingers, I'm in need of a glove who is able to

reach hard-to-get customers; are you interested in $25 an hour?" ...

"Hey you, the glove without a speck of
dirt on it, would you be interested in working
to keep my factory clean?"

So it went. Tyler found the gloves to
fill his factory and loaded them one-by-one
onto the train.

At last he roped a white, wool glove
with a small chain attached to it. Dangling
from the chain was a single charm, the shape
of a heart. Stitched on the glove were the
words, "Start the train."

Tyler and Giselle loaded the cart into
the train and then climbed into the cab
above the engine. "How do we start it? Any
ideas?" Tyler asked Giselle.

They inspected the control panel.
Tyler turned a knob that turned on the
windshield wipers. Giselle flipped a switch

that turned on an overhead light. Tyler pushed a button that honked a loud fog horn. It was so loud it made them jump. Then they giggled.

Then, something caught Giselle's eye. It was a small hole in the control panel that she hadn't noticed during their first inspection. "Look, Tyler, that hole. It's in the shape of a heart."

"A heart? Let me see." Tyler looked to see what Giselle was pointing to. He recognized it and said, "It's a keyhole for the key to start the train,"

"It is?"

"Yes, that heart charm on the last glove I roped—it's the key!"

"You're right, Tyler."

Tyler started the train engine with the heart charm key. The train started moving, leaving a few sparse tumbleweed gloves still tossing in the wind under the blue sky. Giselle and Tyler took their seats in the cab. It wasn't long before the train picked up speed. The train went faster and faster and faster. Before long, they couldn't see anything outside the window but a blur of brown, orange, and blue. The train shook like a washing machine. Giselle and Tyler dug their nails into their chairs trying not to fall out. Then in three seconds, the daylight faded to night. The train roared as it entered a tunnel. It roared on for a few more minutes, then came screeching to a halt. Giselle and Tyler's heads whipped forward then back.

"Ugh. That was a rough ride," Giselle said.

"No kidding. I hope this is the end of it."

They looked out the windows to see they were deep inside a dark tunnel made of dark gray, shiny rock. Off to the right of the train, a spotlight shone down on a steel elevator.

"Look! There's an elevator!" Tyler exclaimed. "We made it to the next elevator!"

"All right!" shouted Giselle.

Tyler grabbed his backpack. Giselle and he hopped off the train and ran for the elevator. The train with the gloves and the cart continued on toward Key Island.

CHAPTER 9:
UNITED TERMITIANS

Tyler checked his e-mail, but there was no new mail. *Hmmm.* Just as he placed the laptop back in the backpack, the elevator doors opened.

"Looks like we have a problem, Tyler." J.J. Junglehammock sat behind a large desk with his feet kicked up and his hands folded under his chin.

Just outside the elevator was J.J.'s small, cozy office. Behind J.J. an exposed brick wall held several black and white photos of forests from the vantage point of the highest tree around. To his right was a window looking out on the city's skyline. To his left a flat screen TV hung between two large bookshelves, mostly filled with law books. In front of J.J.'s desk, a bowl of ripe bananas adorned a small cherry table. Back against the wall to the left of the elevator door, an orange cat slept curled in a perfect circle on the pillow of a plush tan sofa.

"A problem? What kind of problem?"

"Hand me a banana, will ya?" Tyler didn't bother making a comment this time and did as J.J. requested. "The termites, they are ruthless." J.J. peeled his banana and gobbled it down.

"Termites?"

"You can't trust them," he said with his mouth full. "Hand me another banana, will ya?"

"Are you hungry?"

"No, I want to stick it in my armpit and keep it warm." J.J. threw his hands in the air. "Of course, I'm hungry. Now, hand it over, and I'll tell you about these termites."

Growing impatient, Tyler drilled, "Who are these termites?"

"You should know. You hired them to mass produce your Solve-a-matic Machine."

"I did not. I hired hands. I lassoed each one myself," Tyler stuck out his chest with pride.

"Hmmmm." J.J. looked out the window peering into the cityscape. He rested his hands on the window sill and dropped his head between his arms.

"What is it, J.J.?" Giselle tilted her head.

"This looks like a classic case of the Trojan Hand Puppets."

"The what?" asked Tyler.

84

"Did you check under the glove of each hand before you hired them?"

"No, I thought that was against the law?"

"No, no, no. You have every right to check under the glove of each hand. Termites are known to disguise themselves as hands. No telling how many have infiltrated your factory."

"Termites are a hungry bunch. They will eat you out of house and home if you are not careful."

"What?"

"It's a figure of speech, Tyler. Stick with me, will ya?"

J.J. continued, "OK, the leader of the termites, Mr. Silversmith, sent me a letter this morning. Here, read it. Please excuse the banana smudges on the corner."

> We work too many hours,
> But don't get paid enough;
> Change conditions now, or,
> Force us to get rough.
>
> Pay our doctor bills;
> Pay when we retire;
> Make us a great deal,
> Or your fate shall be dire.

"They've gone on strike, Tyler," J.J. turned on the TV behind him. A bar at the bottom of the screen read 4:03 A.M. Behind the reporter they could see termites holding large picket signs and marching in front of Tyler's factory. The factory was completely shut down. No Solve-a-matic Machines would be made today. Anderson Cricket of Action 8 News Channel was reporting on the strike.

> ...Workers unite to protest the long hours and low pay they receive at the Solve-a-matic Factory. Picketers claim they are willing to camp out for weeks to make sure their demands are met. Earlier we spoke with Mr. Silversmith, the leader of the United Termitian Workers. He said the conditions at the factory are awful... Law enforcement officers are trying to keep the strike from turning violent.

"Work too many hours? They work less than the national standard. They get paid twice as much as the average Nessibusian. What more do they want?" Tyler plopped down on the sofa; it almost swallowed him whole. "What are we going to do?"

"Pass me a banana, will ya? OK, this is what you are going to do."

J.J. pulled a pack of large gloves out
of his desk drawer and handed them to
Giselle and Tyler. He told them the plan, and
as his plan unfolded, a look of relief swept
over Tyler's face.

Tyler and Giselle rowed out to the
factory. Termites were picketing everywhere.
Mr. Silversmith, the leader of the
Termitians, had a megaphone. "Our way,
more pay..our way, more pay...," the crowd
chanted.

Tyler approached Mr. Silversmith.
"Excuse me, may we talk for a minute?" Tyler
asked. Mr. Silversmith grumbled something

under his breath that Tyler didn't understand. "What will it take for you to be satisfied with the conditions in the factory?"

"Free chair massages, a big screen TV and an XBox in the break room, two-hour breaks where we still get paid, and double our pay," demanded the leader of the United Termitians Workers.

"Mr. Silversmith, with all due respect, don't you think you're asking for a bit much? You already get paid well above the national average for factory workers and those items in the break room will only serve as a distraction from work."

"No, I do not think it's too much to ask. We are your bread and butter. You need us to keep your factory running."

"I do need you, but Mr. Silversmith, do not be disillusioned to think you are not replaceable. There are many without jobs who would be happy to have yours."

Mr. Silversmith mumbled again.

"I tell you what, I'll give you the free chair massages. I can afford to do that and still keep the factory running. Will that satisfy you?"

Mr. Silversmith was quite stubborn and not willing to compromise. He wanted all his demands or nothing.

Meanwhile, pulling a glove over her head, Giselle went undercover as a Termitian and slipped into the crowd. She saw one termite at the edge of the crowd who didn't look very comfortable. In fact, his picket sign was turned upside-down and resting on his tennis shoes.

Giselle took him aside for a private conversation, and what Giselle discovered, she could not believe. This termite Harmony and many of his friends wanted to be hands, but they couldn't because Mr. Silversmith had the thumb and pinky finger of their gloves tied behind their backs. One might be able to work without their pinky finger, but no one could do much without their thumb.

"I'm going to make you an offer. Hear me out," Giselle whispered.

"Really? Who are you?"

"I'm a friend of your boss, Tyler. He has asked me to talk to you in private."

"Uh, I'm not so sure. Mr. Silversmith would freak if he knew I was talking to you on my own."

"What's your name?"

"Harmony."

"OK, Harmony, I promise it will be worth your while. You see, Tyler tried to deal with Mr. Silversmith, but Mr. Silversmith is being unreasonable. Tyler cannot give anymore without going out of business. So, if you stick with Mr. Silversmith, you can be guaranteed that in a month you will be out of a job; however, I know you are a hard worker, and frankly, Tyler doesn't want to lose you."

"And I don't want to be lost," Harmony said.

Giselle paused at this strange comment, but then chose to ignore it, "So here's the deal. You work as hard as you were working before, and he'll continue to pay you what he's been paying you. You work a little bit harder, and he'll pay you a little bit more. You work really hard and help the factory meet its production goal of building fifty thousand Solve-a-matic Machines by the end of the year, and he'll give you a promotion and double your original pay."

"Wow! That sounds great."

"All of this is under two conditions."

"Which are...?"

"First, you leave United Termitian Workers immediately and release Tyler from his contract with you. Second, you recruit three of your non-union friends and family members, those that are hard workers like you, to come and work here."

"I can do that. But, instead of US dollars, can I get paid in wood chips? I love wood chips," pleaded Harmony.

"I think Tyler can arrange that."

"OK, then it's a deal."

"Terrific," Giselle smiled as she shook his hand. That was easier than she thought. "Here, I have a new glove for you."

So it went. Giselle repeated similar deals, one by one, with each of the best of the United Termitian Workers while Tyler kept Mr. Silversmith occupied. When Giselle had secured enough workers to replace his staff, she signaled to Tyler. Tyler excused himself from Mr. Silversmith and climbed to the second floor landing overlooking the factory floor.

Harmony timidly approached him. "Tyler, I have a gift for you—for being so generous to give me my job back instead of hiring someone else."

"Harmony, you didn't have to..."

"I wanted to. I figured you needed a whistle to blow to get everyone's attention. I noticed you didn't have one."

"You're right, Harmony. I don't have a whistle; I need one."

"Well, I don't have a whistle, but I have something that will work just the same. I want you to have it." Harmony, extended both hands to present Tyler with a harmonica.

"Wow, cool, I've never had a harmonica before. How do you play it?" Harmony showed Tyler how to play a song.

"Let me demonstrate how to make it sound like a whistle. It's best played in the key of G." When Harmony blew the harmonica, the workers saluted from the floor and started up the machines. The building roared with the humming of conveyer belts and the pressure release of pistons. Smoke poured from the factory's stacks once again.

Outside the factory gates, Mr. Silversmith and his stubborn United Termitian Workers stopped chanting, lowered their signs, and dropped their jaws in disbelief. They stood in silence for a few minutes, then they hung their heads and slowly walked away. They had been beaten.

Friends from Tyler's school begin lining up at the gate of the factory. *What did they want?* Tyler wondered. He saw his buddy Jake from the orphanage. "Hi, Jake. What's going on?"

"We heard about your Solve-a-matic Machine. We each came to purchase one. How much are they?"

"Uh, how much are they, hmmmm," Tyler stalled, not knowing what to charge for the Solve-a-matic Machine. "Hang on, while I check something." Tyler walked away from Jake and the crowd. "Soté? Soté, are you there?"

"Hello, Tyler. I'm here," Soté answered.

"I have a problem, Soté. As you can see, my friends are lined up outside ready to purchase the Solve-a-matic Machine, but I don't know what to charge them."

"That sounds like a good problem to have. How much did it cost you to make?"

Tyler added what it cost to run the electricity at his factory, and what it cost to pay his employees, and a few other expenses he had. Then he divided that amount by the number of machines he thought he could make and sell. He came up with $15. "It cost me about $15 to make one machine."

"OK. Now go see what your friends are willing to pay for it. The Solve-a-matic Machine can help them do their homework, too. It's worth some price to them. You will discover the right price by talking to your friend Jake."

Tyler knew what it was worth to himself, but he wasn't sure what it was worth to the kids in line. So he took Soté's advice and approached Jake. "What would you pay for it?"

"Ugh, I don't know." Jake reached for his money in his pocket. He knew he only had $65. It had taken him two weeks of delivering newspapers to earn it. He didn't want to use it all on the Solve-a-matic Machine. "I'll give you $15 for it."

Tyler thought about it. Since it cost him $15 to make a machine, he knew he needed to charge more if he was going to make a profit. So he countered Jake's offer, "It costs $45."

Jake shot back, "Oh, that's too much. I can give you $25 for it."

"For $29.99, it's a deal, Jake. For $29.99 you can have a Solve-a-matic Machine," bargained Tyler.

This time Jake thought about it for a long time. Then, to Tyler's delight, Jake said, "Deal." They shook on it.

Tyler started selling his Solve-a-matic Machines to his friends and his friends' friends for $29.99. In no time he had made enough cash to pay back the money he had borrowed from Soté. After that, he was able to keep his profits. Tyler was becoming rich!

Giselle reminded Tyler that he needed to find a key and finish this round of his journey. Tyler told Giselle he had already found the key. Giselle looked puzzled. Tyler led her back inside the factory to Harmony, his star worker. "Harmony, can you take over selling the Solve-a-matic Machines? I need to step out."

Harmony was honored to take on this important responsibility. Delighted, Tyler pulled the harmonica out of his pocket and asked Harmony to play a song to celebrate the factory's success. Harmony played a fun tune for Giselle and Tyler.

"What song is that?" Tyler asked Harmony.

"It's the song 'Beautiful Dreamer' played in the key of C."

Tyler and Giselle had never heard of that song. It sounded very old, but they agreed there was something catchy about it. Right then elevator doors, which had been disguised in the wall beside them, opened. "See, I told you I had found the key," Tyler said referring to the musical key Harmony played his song in. "Thanks, Harmony. Come on, Giselle. Let's go." They jumped on the elevator and up it went.

CHAPTER 10:
CRUNCHING ICE,
CRUNCHING NUMBERS

Many a bean to build your machine;
Replace your sack of red with black;

Seek service of snow that slumbers,
To guard you from Crunching Numbers.

Hmmmm. Replace your sack of red with black...and Crunching Numbers. "What do you think all of this means, Giselle?"

The elevator doors opened. A cold, sharp wind rushed in sending a chill up

Tyler's spine. The sky was gray. The snow was gray. It was hard to tell where the snow and sky met on the horizon. Snowflakes circled around like dancers competing in a waltz. Squinting his eyes Tyler could barely make out a red sign stuck in the snow. The sign pointed left of a snow drift.

Tyler headed off in the direction of the sign. "I wish we had some snow boots and coats right now," Tyler yelled back at Giselle, who was trying to keep up with him.

"Yeah, my shoes are getting wet, and I'm freezing."

"Hey, look! It's a cave."

"Cool! Let's go explore."

The cave was dark and slippery. Ice covered the walls and the ceiling. Muddy slush covered most of the floor except in a few spots where stone broke through. The only source of light came from gas lanterns that hung twenty feet apart on alternating sides of the cave walls. Ahead of Tyler and Giselle were three dark, cold paths. Before them sat a pile of red kidney beans.

"Look, *'many a bean to build your machine, replace your sack of red with black'*. Just like the riddle says—a million-ga-zillion red beans."

"You're right, Tyler. Look, over there," Giselle pointed to a wall on their right, "a bunch of old burlap sacks are hanging on the wall."

Above each path was a sign. One read 'Gold Paint This Way." One read 'Silver Paint This Way.' The last one read 'Black Paint This Way.'

"Well, the riddle mentions replacing the sack of red with black. So, I'm going to guess that we need to pack the red beans in as many sacks as we can carry, follow that path," Tyler pointed to the one marked for black paint, "and drop them in the black paint when we find it."

Giselle looked down the murky path where shadows fluttered with the flickering light. "If we find it."

"Oh Giselle, don't be silly. We'll find it. Don't worry, I'm sure it's there."

"I'm not worried that it's not there. I'm just afraid of what else might be between here and there, lurking in the shadows."

"Well, I can't worry about that. It's 5:10 A.M. I have just a little more than an hour before the sun rises, and if I haven't figured out how to turn my red beans to black, then it's all over for me. I don't have time to worry."

Off in the distance, a bat screeched. Giselle raised her eyebrows at Tyler. Tyler shrugged and started to fill sacks with red beans.

They carried as many red beans as they could. They grabbed the first lantern off the wall to light their way. The slushy ice crunched as it gave way to the weight of their loads.

CRASH! "What was that? Shine the lantern." Tyler did, but the path ahead was completely dark.

"I'm scared, Tyler," quivered Giselle.

"Oh, it's nothing." Tyler continued into the darkness. "So, the riddle said, '*Seek service of snow that slumbers, To guard you from Crunching Numbers.*' What do you suppose that means?" he asked.

"I don't know. Sounds like gibberish to me." Giselle grabbed Tyler's arm and walked a little closer to him. She did not want to be far from the light.

"I'm stumped. This riddle is not making much sense to me."

CRASH!

"Aghhhh!" even Tyler jumped this time and stopped dead in his tracks.

"Tyler?" Giselle squeezed Tyler's arm even tighter.

"Shhh!" Tyler lifted his lamp up to see the top of a large opening in the cave—a ballroom with ice walls. Hanging from the top, like chandeliers, were beautiful icicles, glistening, gleaming. "Look, Giselle. The icicles are shaped like numbers."

"Look," Giselle pointed to the ceiling above her right side, "There are Twos over there."

"Over here are the Fives," Tyler and Giselle stood in awe under the ceiling of ice crystal numbers. One through nine, they all were represented. In the middle of the room were gold zeroes, whose radiant color and sheer size commanded the reverence of the other numbers.

Just then, a cracking sound came from above. They looked up just in time to see a large Four break away from the ceiling and freefall towards them.

"Look out!" Giselle grabbed Tyler who then lost hold of his lantern. The lantern went crashing to the ground, but Giselle and Tyler leapt out of the way and fell into the slush together. They looked back and saw their bags of red beans still sitting in the middle of the ballroom. The Four crashed down right where they had been standing. "Shwew! That was close."

"So these are the Crunching Numbers that the riddle mentions." Another crack from above echoed.

"Let's get out of here!" They ran back to the edge of the room as numbers began crashing down all around them. They had no time to go get their beans, they needed to save their lives.

After reaching cover at the edge of the ballroom and taking a few minutes to catch their breath, Giselle asked, "What are we going to do? Now we're separated from our red beans, and this black paint is no-where in site."

"Zzzzzzzzzzzz."

"Did you hear that, Tyler?" whispered Giselle.

"Yeah, it sounds like it's coming from over there. Loud obnoxious snoring was resonating from a dark gap in the cave corridors.

"Zzzzzzzzzzz."

"Come on. Let's check it out."

"I'm not going in there," Giselle shook her head. "It's pitch black."

"OK, suit yourself. I'm going. You can stay here, or you can join me. Your choice."

"Zzzzzzzzzzz."

An Eight at the edge of the icicle ballroom came crashing down beside them—too close for comfort. "OK, OK, I'm coming."

Following the vibrations of the snoring, they came to a fork in the path. Sleeping against the cave wall that separated the two paths was a large, polar bear. The fur on the top of his head was spiked and dyed yellow. His round glasses had fallen from his nose and dangled off his right ear. A small black calculator clung for its life on his belly, rising and falling to the rhythm of his breathing like a doomed raft on an icy ocean.

"Yikes," whispered Giselle. The bear's snoring stopped midstream. Giselle and Tyler froze. For a solid minute, neither of them moved, not even to blink.

"Hey. The riddle said something about slumber. What was it, do you remember?" Tyler said softly.

"It said, 'Seek the service of something that slumbers.'"

"Was it a "bear that slumbers?"

"Zzzzzzzzzzz."

"I, uh, don't think so. It was something like sleet or snow."

Snapping his fingers, "That's it."

The bear stopped snoring again, but this time he shifted, and his dangling glasses dropped to the iced-covered stone floor. Dink. The calculator still balanced on his belly.

"That's it," Tyler continued, "'Seek service of snow that slumbers, to guard you from Crunching Numbers.' He's our slumbering snow."

"He's not snow; he's a bear."

"Yeah, but he looks like snow, and he sure is slumbering."

"OK, you may be right, but you aren't going to wake him, are you? I'm not going over there."

"Chicken."

"That's right, one live chicken. Better to be that than a dead man walking."

"Thanks."

"Why are you tiptoeing when you are going to wake him anyway? What difference does it make? Wouldn't it make sense to make a loud noise from afar?"

He spun around with cross eyes, "You talk too much, Giselle. Can you be quiet for just a second?"

Giselle crossed her arms and slid her back down the wall of ice behind her. She landed Indian style on the stone floor.

"Excuse me," Tyler said timidly.

The bear kept snoring.

"Excuse me," Tyler called a little louder. The bear stopped snoring but continued to sleep. Tyler tapped him on his arm. "I said, 'Excuse me.'"

"What, what?" The bear sat up; his eyes half open. The calculator slipped to the floor. The bear looked to the left then found Tyler on his right. He rubbed his eyes then moved in close to get a better look at Tyler while he fumbled to find his spectacles. "Who are you?"

"I'm Tyler. I've come to replace my red beans with black ones. Only I can't find the black paint, and I'm afraid it may be on the other side of the Crunching Numbers, which are crashing down all around us making it very difficult. The worse part of it all is that the sacks of red beans are stranded in the middle of the roo..."

The bear interrupted, "Hold on, child. Slow down. Take a breath and start again, but more slowly this time." Tyler told the bear his story again, more slowly.

Afterwards, the bear said he could help. He was an accountant, and he explained that accountants know their way through the crunching numbers' room. They know the unmarked paths. "Legal paths, of course," he explained.

"Legal? Why wouldn't they be legal."

"Some cave paths are off limits," the bear pointed to a cave path twenty feet away. "No Trespassing," "Keep Out," and "Danger," signs surrounded the entrance. "Like that one over there. The bats lurk in the dark shadows of those paths. It's best not to disturb the bats. Let them sleep."

The polar bear picked up his glasses from the ground and cleaned the smudges off with his fur. "Now follow me, and I'll show you the way."

They returned to the ballroom of crunching numbers. Numbers continued to crash down all around them. They could see the sacks of red beans sitting in the middle of the room. The bear stopped to tell them the rules of the game.

"When a 1 falls in your path, you slide 1 step to the left. When a 2 falls in your path, you slide 2 steps to the right. When a 3 falls in your path, you take 3 steps forward. When a 4 falls in your path, you go 3 steps forward and 1 to the right or left. When a 5 falls in your path, you run straight all the way to the wall. When a 6 falls in your path, you do 6 summersaults in a row. When a 7 falls in your path, hop on 1 foot 7 times, diagonally. When an 8 falls in your path, do a cartwheel. When a 9 falls in your path, crawl on you belly 9 times. When a 0 falls in your path, do NOT move. Got it?"

"No, that's too much to remember. I can't remember it. I'm going to get killed," Tyler shook his head intensely.

The crunching numbers terrified Tyler. They reminded him of how his father died, being crushed by a boat. Fear paralyzed him.

"You can do it, Tyler," Giselle said as she squeezed Tyler's hand.

Then a 3 crashed down. "What was 3?" Tyler asked the polar bear.

"Take 3 steps forward," the bear replied.

So, Tyler took 3 steps forward. Then a 7 crashed down right in front of him, nearly taking off his nose. "What's 7? I forgot 7!" he panicked.

The polar bear started to tell him to hop on one foot seven times, but before the bear could finish speaking, a 4 came crashing down in Tyler's path. It shattered, and a piece of it flew up and hit Tyler in the arm. "Ouch!" Tyler jumped back to the edge of the ballroom out of harms way. "I can't do it. It's too fast."

"You can, but you can't wait for me to direct you. You have to learn each number yourself, so you can react quickly."

Memorizing the steps, the image of his father's death, and the threat of the crashing numbers was more than Tyler could handle. "I can't do it."

The polar bear said, "Tyler, you've come a long way to get this far. You are so close to fulfilling your dreams. However, you've only gone 95% of the way. To stand out from the rest—to realize your dream of becoming a successful entrepreneur—you must finish the race, that last 5%, your last task. It's all the way, or you get nothing. Without turning your red beans to black, Tyler, you get nothing. Do you understand what's at stake here?"

Tyler bowed his head and wiped a tear from his eye. "Then, I guess I'm not an entrepreneur after all because I just can't go back in there."

Giselle looked away. She couldn't bear to see it all come to this.

The polar bear eyes changed from sympathetic to stern, "Then I guess you're not, Tyler." The bear shook his head, "I guess you're not. If you cannot finish the journey, then you must turn back and take the path that leads back to your orphanage."

"I have to go back?"

"You can't live here," the bear said. Tyler looked around at the cold dark caves and then looked into the ballroom of crunching numbers. "Yes, sir," Tyler lowered his head in shame and fought back more tears. He looked up at Giselle, who stood motionless in disbelief.

"Come on, Tyler. You can do this. I know you can," pleaded Giselle.

"I can't, Giselle. I just can't. Goodbye, Giselle." Giselle was so angry with Tyler, she could not even look at him or say goodbye.

Tyler, with his backpack strapped to his back and his head hanging low, took the path leading back to the orphanage. A rickety, metal elevator awaited him. Above it a sign said, "Point of No Return". Tyler thought about the sweat and blood he had put into designing and building his Solve-a-matic Machine. He thought about those pesky pirate parrots who tried to copy his plans and how he fought to get them back. He thought about his factory and the perfect land it sits on. He thought about all the hands working there depending on him for a job. He thought about his dream to sail a-round the world, and he remembered his dreadful days at the orphanage. He stepped on the elevator and pushed the button to go down. Then Tyler thought about his father, the man he never knew. *Maybe for the better*, Tyler thought, *he'd be disappointed.*

But then something inside Tyler stirred. This did not feel right. He could not live with regrets; he could not wonder the rest of his life what might have been. That was more unbearable than facing the crunching numbers. Just before the doors to the elevator closed, Tyler threw his arm in their path. With all his strength, he pried the doors back open.

The doors sprang back; he jumped off. He wasted no time. He ran back down the path towards the crunching numbers' ballroom. But when he arrived, he saw neither the polar bear nor Giselle. Where had they gone? The sacks of beans were right where he had left them. He didn't know exactly what time it was, but he knew he had to hurry. *What were those rules again?* "Here I go."

Tyler ran into the room straight towards his sacks of red beans. He picked-up what he could just before an eight crashed down in front of him. "Eight, oh yeah, a cartwheel. I'm supposed to do a cartwheel." This was a tricky move with sacks of beans in his hand and a backpack on his back, but he managed. Just as soon as he did, a nine crashed down beside him. He dropped to his belly and crawled right up to a crashing zero, dragging the sacks with him. He did not make a move until a five crashed down next. He jumped up and ran straight ahead to the wall. So it went on for fifteen minutes. Tyler was getting exhausted, but he looked up after a crawl and saw another path with the sign 'Black Paint This Way.' He had made it through the crunching numbers! He ran down the dimly lit path to a small round room with a whirlpool of black paint in the center.

"I knew you'd come back." Giselle walked out of the shadows.

"I couldn't leave, Giselle. It didn't feel right."

"Let's turn these red beans to black."

The black paint was as thick as oil and swirled slowly in the whirlpool. One bat above them opened an eye and raised his eyebrow in suspicion. They froze with fear, afraid he'd try to attack them, but he just watched with an icy stare. So, they dumped their red beans and watched them disappear. The beans left behind glowing spots on the surface where they had plunged. Seconds later the beans popped back to the surface. They were black.

Then a funny thing happened. Each black bean lit on fire. Little flames were burning all over the whirlpool. Then all of a sudden, the whole whirlpool went up in a large flame, creating a massive bonfire. Tyler and Giselle jumped back, for the heat was intense.

The fire started to melt the ice on the cave ceiling and the wall beside them. On the other side of the wall of melting ice, an elevator awaited them.

CHAPTER 11:
THE PENTHOUSE

The elevator was made of glass windows. There was nothing to see beyond the windows but the dark gray stone wall of the cave. Once they were ascending, the walls beyond the windows gave way to the city lights against the dark sky. The elevator left the lower stories of the building and rode along the side of the uppermost stories.

"Look, Tyler, the sun is rising."

They watched a beautiful display of the sun's arching red rays pushing up the pre-dawn sky. Buildings to the west, reflecting the red light on each window, created the illusion of an entire city made of burning coal embers. Higher and higher they climbed up the needle of the building, until finally the elevator slowed to a stop.

"Congratulations, Tyler."

"Soté?"

"Yes, Tyler. I'm here." Tyler looked a-round, but couldn't see the source of the voice. "You have reached the top floor of the building."

"Do you live here, Soté?"

"No, my child. I'm here to congratulate you. You will now reap the rewards of your labor. You have succeeded in creating your Solve-a-matic company before sunrise. You have learned many lessons along the way. You have found your confidence, learned to be organized, and devoted yourself to your work. You have learned to be resourceful and have unleashed your imagination on the world. You've learned to lead, and you've learned to take risks. Tuck these experiences away in your memory bank. You are going to need them in future endeavors."

"Future endeavors?"

"Yes, Tyler. You are now an entre-preneur."

"I am?"

"Yes, you are. Once it gets in your blood, you can never stop. It is a way of life that few succeed at, but those who do, embrace it for life. Yes, Tyler, there will be many future endeavors for you."

"Now, you have worked hard, and it's time for you to rest a little and cash in on the dream that sustained you throughout this journey. So, go now and see what awaits you."

The doors sprung open. The word 'PENTHOUSE' in large spotless brass letters hung over two interior, glass doors, etched with an image of Earth. In front of the glass doors, laid out on an antique table, like the one he found on the first floor elevator with the creative juice smoothies, were all the items from his cart: the Solve-a-matic Machine, his blueprint plans, and the beautiful treasure chest.

"Oh, pretty," Giselle said admiring the treasure chest. She walked over to open it.

"It's locked. I tried it."

"You've seen it before?"

"Yeah, I tripped over it in the rain forest where I lost you."

Ignoring Tyler, Giselle tried to open the chest, and to Tyler's surprise, it opened. Tyler ran over to see what was inside.

"The photo of my father! I thought I'd lost it." Tyler scooped up the photo and studied it as he had a thousand times.

"He's handsome, Tyler...like you." Tyler blushed as he quickly stole a glance at Giselle's smile and returned his gaze back to his father's photo. Underneath the photo was a golden key.

"You know, Giselle, I could not have made it here without you. You know that, don't you?"

"I know. Thanks for saying so."

"Well, do you want to see what lies behind this final door?"

"I thought you'd never ask."

Tyler took the golden key and inserted it into the keyhole of the Earth-etched glass doors. A rooftop terrace with vine-laced trellises shaded lounge chairs on each side. An Earth-shaped pool with latitude and longitude lines painted on the bottom divided the trellises. At the other end of the terrace, a green and yellow hot-air balloon was tied down to the building.

"Wow!" Tyler could not contain his excitement. He ran over and jumped in the balloon. Giselle joined him, and together they rode the balloon through the city. The morning sun rested on the blue Bay of Nessibus. When the balloon finally came to rest, they found themselves before a large docked yacht.

"Wow, a boat like my father's!" Tyler gazed at every inch of the ship. It was big, bright, and white. The shiny deck was made of the finest polished wood. The American flag flapped in the breeze.

Soté's voice spoke, "This is yours. You have earned it."

"It's mine to keep?"

"To keep."

"I can sail around the world now." Eagerly, Tyler climbed down from the dock into the boat. The floor in the back of the boat was covered in envelopes. He picked one up, opened it and read the letter. Then he read another one, and then another. Each letter was from a different child who lived somewhere in the world. Each thanked Tyler for creating the Solve-a-matic Machine to help them do their homework faster. "Cool," Tyler exclaimed softly to himself.

Then he looked back at Giselle, who was running her hand along the beautiful polished wood paneling. Her long hair blew in the wind. To Tyler, she never looked more beautiful than she did at this moment.

"Giselle, I'm going to set sail."

"Now?"

"Why not?"

"How long will you be gone?"

"I don't know. A week? A month? Maybe even a year."

"A year? Then who's going to run the factory?" Although Giselle kept a glassy smile on her face, the slightest wrinkle surfaced between her young eyes, and Tyler could tell she was trying to hide her disappointment in the length of their separation.

"I was hoping you'd do that for me. I'll pay you well."

Giselle looked away in thought. "Hmmm, I could do that. Yeah. I'll run your factory until you return. If you ever return."

"I'll be back to start more businesses, Giselle. I'm an entrepreneur now, you know. It's in my blood."

"I know." Giselle knew that he was right.

And with that, Tyler started the engine of the yacht and waved goodbye. Giselle waved back. Just as Tyler was about to pull away, he called out, "Hey, Giselle. I'll call Harmony. He can run my factory for me while I'm gone. Why don't you join me?"

"Really?" Giselle's voice perked up.

"Really."

"I need to ask my mom."

"Call her when we get to the next port," Tyler suggested.

"OK!"

After Giselle had joined Tyler on the boat, and they had pulled out of the harbor, Tyler turned to Giselle and asked, "If Şoté doesn't live on that top floor, which one does he live on?"

"Tyler, he doesn't live in that building."

"He doesn't?" Tyler thought for a moment, but couldn't make sense of it. Soté knew the building so well. He was there all the time. The building had many residential floors. "Then where does he live?"

Giselle sat down in a lounge chair on deck, took a sip of lemonade, and smiled. "In you, Tyler. Soté lives in you."

◆ THE END ◆

7871187R0

Made in the USA
Lexington, KY
20 December 2010